ABOUT THE AUTHOR

Christopher Oyo is Ugandan born and bred.
A good part of his evenings as a child were
spent listening to traditional folk stories and
riddles. Stories told by parents who heard it from their
parents who heard it from their parents, who heard it
from their parents...

Christopher lives in London with his wife and their
two daughters aged 7 and 10, who he continuously
hassles with folk stories he heard from his parents.

ABOUT THE ILLUSTRATOR

Charity Russell is Zambian born and grew up mostly
in South Africa and Australia. She moved to the U.K.
as a teenager, and now lives in Bristol, England
with her husband, two children aged 10 and 20 and their dog
Frank.

she loves a good folk tale and loves to tell stories,
she's very good at scary ones!

This book belongs to

....

To Alicia, Ash, Libby
Blessings Always.

IT'S FINDERS KEEPERS

By Christopher Oyo

Art by Charity Russell

Long ago, in faraway lands, animals were always arguing.

It was one argument and fallout after the other.

This did not please his Royal Highness the King.

He made a new rule, which he hoped would stop some of the bickering within the kingdom.

'As to property unowned or abandoned, it's finders keepers,' declared the king.

'What does this mean?' the animals asked.

'It means, if you leave any of your things lying around, whoever finds it may keep it,' King Lion roared.

The rule was music to Crocodile's ears.
Big plans formed in her mischievous head.
'What a king-given opportunity this is?!'
she thought. 'It's about time I found out
what it's like to sleep on fur!'

One afternoon as Hare was out hunting, Crocodile hurried to Hare's burrow and grabbed the fluffy fur that made his bed. On her way out, she bellowed loudly to say the fur was hers. 'Finders keepers!'

Hare was worried when he heard the bellows of Crocodile. He ran out of the woods and saw Crocodile had his fluffy fur bedding.

'How dare you, can I have my fur back, please?' Hare hissed.

'The fur is now mine,' Crocodile growled.

Back and forth the two animals tussled over ownership of the fur.

Suddenly the king's voice boomed out at them from the woods.

'It's finders keepers, animals.'

The victorious Crocodile slithered away happily with a smile on her face and the fur bedding on her back.

Hare was furious and thought of ways to get his fur bedding back.

He did not have to wait long.

Early the next day as Crocodile crawled off from the riverbank and into the warm water for a bath.

Hare rushed into Crocodile's den, but there was no sign of his fur bedding, he instead grabbed Crocodile's eggs and left the den, juggling the eggs with excitement.

'I have found myself some lovely crocodile eggs,' he crooned.

Crocodile heard the commotion and quickly swam onto the shore.

'What are you doing with my eggs?' she asked Hare.

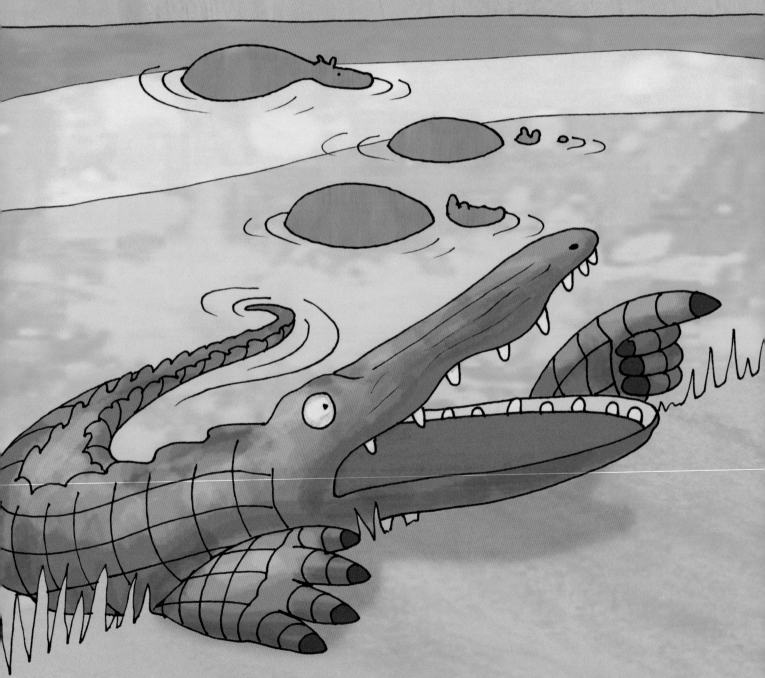

'I now own these eggs,' said Hare. 'But you can have your eggs back if you give me my fur.' Crocodile thought about Hare's offer and said, 'No.'
'This is not over!' Hare declared.

The next day, Hare woke up grumpy. He had not slept well without his bedding.

What else can I take from Crocodile to make her give me my fur back? Hare wondered.

He noticed lots of twigs around Crocodile's den.

'I might as well use them to make my bed.'

Hare picked up the twigs and carried them to his home.

He did not realise that a very angry Crocodile was following him!

'Give me back my eggs and twigs!'
Crocodile demanded.

Hare jumped in surprise, answering.
'Only after you have given back my
fur.'

'No way.' Crocodile growled.

As days went by, Crocodile struggled to sleep. She realised that Hare's fur bedding was not as warm as she had thought it would be, it was too small and made her sneeze...

Her nose would not stop itching.

Over in Hare's burrow, he too could not sleep. Lying on Crocodile's twigs was not comfortable. They were prickly and the eggs were starting to hatch.

'It was a bad idea bringing Crocodile's things to my burrow,' Hare decided.

He scooped up the baby crocodiles, twigs and the last of the eggs, and hurried towards Crocodile's home.

Bam!! He ran straight into Crocodile, who was hurriedly crawling towards him with his fur bedding on her back.

'You can have your things back!!' they said to each other at the same time.

Hare gratefully took his fur and Crocodile took her babies, eggs, and twigs.

'I'm sorry for taking your fur, Hare,' said Crocodile.

'And I shouldn't have taken your things in revenge, Crocodile,' answered Hare.

The two shook hands and agreed never to take each other's things again.

Printed in Great Britain
by Amazon